Not So   Four

THE FAMOUS FIVE

by Michaela Morgan
Illustrated by Mick Reid

WELCOME

LONGMAN

CONTENTS

CHAPTER 1
Holidays

"That's that then," said Karen staring at the list. "We've read every single one – some of them twice."

"Or three times," said Kristina.

"Or four ..."

"Or more!"

"So what are we going to do now?" Kristina's plump face was the picture of misery. She was batty about Blyton. She'd read every Secret Seven, every Famous Five and anything else by Enid Blyton that she could find.

Now she'd run out. There were no new ones left to read.

Nothing to read.

Nothing to do.

Nowhere to go.

The long summer holidays stretched ahead. It was only the first day and already everything was BORING!

The two trudged back to Karen's house. Kristina's Mum and Dad ran the chip shop and worked all hours. They lay around as pale and pasty as uncooked cod all morning.

They stayed in bed as long as they could, then dragged themselves up and ran around panicking about the lunchtime rush. Then they collapsed again and even snoozed in the afternoon given half a chance.

Tiptoeing around and shushing each other all the time was no fun, so Kristina hung around with Karen as much as she could. Six weeks of hanging around and being quiet – it didn't bear thinking about.

Kristina sat on the squishy bean bag in Karen's room. "Got anything new to play with?" she asked hopefully. But no, there was only the usual assortment of junk:

ancient jigsaws missing half their pieces;

Monopoly without the paper money or the lucky Scottie dog;

an over-brushed and balding My Little Pony;

and a collection of old Sindy and Barbie dolls long past their best.

Karen was getting too old for toys, or so she said, so nobody bought her new ones. Finding anything to play with at her house was going to be a bit of a challenge.

"I'll go and see what's on the telly," said Kristina. She was back soon. "Cricket test match," she sighed. "Three days of it! Or golf ... or black and white films and Playbus."

They sank into gloom.

"This never happened to the Famous Five," sighed Kristina. "They never hung around being bored. What would they do? What would the Secret Seven do?"

"They'd have a meeting," said Karen. "They'd have a meeting and they'd find an adventure, that's what!"

"Well, why don't we do that too?" said Kristina.

CHAPTER 3
The Daring Duo

"We could call ourselves the Daring Duo or ..."

"The Terrific Two or ..."

"The Krazy Kristina and Karen!"

"We'll look out for crooks to catch and smugglers to foil. We'll keep our eyes open for clues and our ears open for ..."

"KAREN!"

A rude interruption to all their thoughts and plans came in the shape of Karen's mum. "I've left you a snack. I've got to go out for a couple of hours. James is supposed to be here to look after you. Where is that boy? While you wait for him you're not to answer the door to anyone. You know the rules Karen. What are they?"

Karen sighed and chanted, "I'm not to answer the phone. I'm not to open the door to anyone and I'm not to go out."

"Right," said her mum. "You just wait here till your big brother arrives to look after you. Okay?"

And she was off.

Kristina ate most of Karen's snack. Very little put her off food - not even disappointment. "Fat chance of any adventure," she mumbled through a cheese and pickle sandwich, "if we're not allowed to even open the door!"

"Mmm. We've got a problem," admitted Karen. "The real Famous Five could travel all over the countryside. I'm not even allowed to go to the park without my mum or my brother. Mum says it isn't safe."

"It's not fair," Kristina complained. "The Famous Five could row off to mysterious islands, explore deserted houses and caves. All I'm allowed to do is come round to your house."

"And we haven't got one single secret passage here," said Karen. "We haven't even got a loft! It's hopeless. How are we ever going to have an adventure if we can't go anywhere by ourselves? Would you mind a lot if my mum came with us?" she asked, hopefully.

"Of course I'd mind!" said Kristina. "The Dynamic Duo and their Mums! Doesn't have quite the same dashing ring, does it?"

"What we need ..." sighed Karen, "is someone older. Someone Mum trusts ... someone like ..."

"Your big brother James!"

"Jaz! Yeah! He's practically grown up. We'll ask Jaz. We'll let him join our gang."

CHAPTER 4
The Thrilling Three

"We could call ourselves the Thrilling Three," the girls explained to Jaz. "We'd have loads of adventures. Mum would let me go if you came too, because you're big."

"Too big," said Jaz. "Too big for your kiddy games."

"We'd be no trouble," wheedled Karen.

"No chance. No how. No way," said Jaz. "No!" And he plugged his ears into his Walkman and closed his eyes.

So that was the end of that – or was it?

At teatime Karen's mum came home.

"Cup of tea!" she gasped, sinking into the chair. "I got it!" she announced.

"Got what?" said Karen. "The flu?"

"No, twitto, the job," said Jaz. "Mum's been for an interview."

"Sorry I didn't tell you love," Mum smiled apologetically at Karen. "I wasn't sure I had much chance of getting this job. It's a really good one. Just what I wanted – good money too. Only one problem ..."

"Yeah?" said Jaz. "And that is?"

"I have to start straight away – even though it's the holidays. Time for a drink and a discussion."

So they started with a drink and a discussion. Then they went on to chocolate biscuits and complaining and finally settled for pocket money and persuading. The plan they worked out and agreed was this:

"No excuses!" said Mum. "It can't be done any other way. Karen is too big for babysitters and too young to be left on her own. There's no point me working if I have to pay someone to look after her. I know neither of you like it but it's just for the summer and with all the money I earn we'll do something to make up for it."

"What?" asked Jaz, sulkily.

"A proper holiday," his mum promised. "Just as soon as I've earned enough money. We haven't had a holiday away for years."

CHAPTER 5

"So, as you're stuck with me anyway, you might as well join our club," insisted Karen, the next day. Jaz, worn down and fed up, wearily agreed. "Oh all right – but only if I'm the leader."

"It was my idea ..." Karen started to object but Kristina hissed at her, "Just pretend he's the leader if it makes him feel better."

"And only," he added, "if one of *my* friends can join too. So we'll have to be the something four. What about the Not So Famous Four?"

So that's what happened. The first meeting was held by the old coal bunker at the bottom of the garden. They voted to let Bharat join. "You'll be glad you asked me," he said. "I've got loads of ideas!"

Karen had more than ideas. She had a notebook and pencil. She opened it importantly. "We should have special names," she said.

"Like ...?"

"Like Black Hand," said Bharat, "or Screech Owl or Spirit Snapper or Werewolf or ..."

"Or Tina," said Kristina. She'd always wanted people to call her Tina but they always forgot. Somehow she looked just too *big* to be anything less than her full name.

"And a password," said Karen. "We need a password and badges."

"And a secret code," added Bharat, "and identity cards and a proper secret meeting place and ..."

"Hang on," said Karen. "One thing at a time. Names."

"Don't be bossy!" said Jaz. "I'm the leader, remember."

Karen sighed. "All right," she said sweetly, "you can choose the names."

"I'm Jaz of course," he was proud of his nickname. "Bharat can be Baz. Karen can be Kaz." Then he looked at Kristina. "I'll call you ... Fatty."

Kristina went pink.

"You can call me Kaz," said Karen. "I like it. But we'll call Kristina ... Tina. That's her name and," she added loyally, "it's a very pretty name too! So that's agreed then," and she ticked it off the list she was making. For someone who wasn't the leader she certainly took charge.

"Next proposal?" she asked.

"We ought to have an animal," said Baz. "A loyal faithful dog."

"Yes," agreed Tina. "All gangs have an animal – a parrot or a monkey or ..."

"A dog," insisted Baz.

"Or a dog," she said.

"We've got a hamster at home," said Jaz.

"Get real! Who's ever heard of a hero and his hamster!" crowed Baz.

"It can do tricks," Karen added loyally.

"Oh yeah! Like rounding up crooks and terrifying smugglers I suppose!"

"Like swinging on its bars and running round its wheel," said Kaz. "It's really good at that."

"No, it won't do!" said Jaz. "Baz is right. We need a dog. How can we get a dog?"

CHAPTER 6
First mission

"I'm not allowed to keep a dog," said Tina. "We live in a flat above the shop. We've got a budgie but ..."

"Exactly," said Jaz. "A budgie won't do either."

"There's a house down our road with dogs," said Baz. "Loads of dogs. They're always barking. We could borrow one of theirs. Told you I had loads of ideas," he smirked.

"Right!" said Karen. "That will be one of our first missions – won't it?" she added, tactfully looking at Jaz.

"That will be our second mission," he ordered. "First we organise our equipment. Make a list."

He lay back in the sun and dictated: "Notebooks and pencils – for noting clues ..." Everyone chipped in and in the end the list looked like this:

Notebook, Pencils.
Torch.
Rope or string
(to tie baddies up)
Food (for secret
feasts).
Binoc Binocc
Binoculars.
And special badges.

"Right," said Jaz. "Now, for the moment, our base will be here by this bush. I'm going to give you your missions. Return here by ... 16.30."

"Half past four," muttered Baz.

"I'll organise you all from here," said Jaz and he plugged his Walkman back in and lay back on the grass. "Now clear off!"

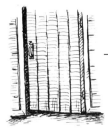

CHAPTER 7
A meeting place

The two girls went over to Kristina's house. They had no problem finding food. She lived in a chip shop after all. There were cans and cans of cola, boxes of crisps, cartons of KitKats, and no end of leftover bits and pieces.

"It's okay," said Kristina. "I'm allowed to take as much as I want." No wonder she was a bit on the plumpish side.

There was no problem with the notebooks either. Tina had loads of bits of leftover exercise books and the two girls ripped them up and folded them into small notebook shapes, held together with elastic bands. Then they helped themselves to four of Tina's felt tips, and that was done. The rope was more difficult to track down but finally they found a car tow-rope at the back of the garage and borrowed that.

"Why do you have a tow-rope when you haven't got a car?" asked Kaz.

"Dunno," said Tina. "It was already in the garage when we came here. I suppose you might as well ask why we have a garage when we haven't got a car but it's useful for keeping ..."

"Got it!" said Kaz. "This can be the den. Look there's

all sorts of stuff we can use to make it homely. And no one comes in here, do they?"

"Brill!" said Tina. "And it won't be far for me to carry things from the house. I'll go and ask Dad if it's okay."

In no time at all she was staggering back to the garage with her arms full. "I've got a brush for cleaning up," she said, "and some old cushions Mum said I could have. Plus some posters and paper and stuff from my room and Dad says we can have some of these boxes – we can sit on them."

Kaz and Tina had fun arranging everything. They turned the boxes upside down and put a cushion on each one. They even put two together to make a sort of sofa. They swept the worst cobwebs away but saved plenty of the cleaning jobs for the boys.

"We can't let them get away with doing nothing," said Kaz. Tina was busy thinking how she could make a shelf when suddenly

EEEEOWWWW

an ear-splitting screech made them jump.

"W-W-What was that?" stammered Kaz, when it finally stopped. "It sounded like ... like ... a screaming spook."

"Or a howling werewolf …"

"Or … a dalek in pain?"

"Like nothing I've ever heard. Spooky."

"Let's go back to the others," suggested Tina, nervously. "We've got practically everything now anyway. We've done really well." They ran off.

Meanwhile, Baz was having a bit of difficulty with his mission. He was standing outside the door of number eighty-six listening with a sinking heart to the assorted bayings, growlings and scratchings coming from inside. Suddenly he was not all that sure he wanted a dog.

He took a deep breath and gave a timid knock. It was like taking the top off a volcano. Dogs hurled themselves at the door, snapping and growling. A huge voice shouted "WHAT D'YA WANT? GO AWAY!" Baz ran.

He met Kaz and Tina skipping back. "Mission accomplished," they reported. "What about you?"

"There was no one in," lied Baz, but he was a bad liar. His ears went red and practically lit up.

"Hmmm," said Kaz, "we'll all go round and ask together."

So that's what they did.

CHAPTER 8
Four-legged fiends

Kaz, Baz, Jaz and Tina stood outside the door and gazed at the flaking paint. Behind the door the dogs were breathing – loudly.

"I didn't know anything could breathe as loud as that," whispered Karen. "They must be monsters."

Even Jaz looked less than certain. He was just thinking of suggesting they trained the hamster up instead when a hand came down on his shoulder.

"Just what do you kids think you're up to then?" said a gruff voice.

Kaz, Baz, Jaz and Tina all spun round and trembled. If there had been an Olympic synchronised trembling event they would have won the gold medal – no contest.

It was Kaz who got her wits back first. "We came to see if you wanted your dogs walking ... sort of good deed," she quavered.

"It doesn't matter though," said Baz quickly. "You're probably busy ..."

"You want to walk my dogs? That's the idea, is it?" asked the man.

Baz was backing away. "Don't worry we can ask someone else," he stammered.

"It's not a bad idea." The man scratched his stubbly chin. "Might quieten 'em down. All right, come and meet my four-legged fiends."

"Fiends! Doesn't he mean 'friends'?" whispered Kaz.

"Hope so," said Baz, staring wide-eyed as the door swung open.

"We'll just wait out here," said Jaz. He knew better than to go into a stranger's house. "We can see them from here."

The kids stood on the step and peered in nervously. In the cramped, dark hall, pairs of glowing eyes gleamed.

"There they are!" said the man. "My best dog is Bruno."

"Is that because he's brown and cuddly like a teddy bear?" asked Karen, hopefully.

"No. It's because he's a boxer," said the man. "Like Frank Bruno. Only bigger."

It was the ugliest, slobberiest, smelliest dog you could imagine. Each paw was about the size of a sliced loaf and from his mouth a constant stream of drool slobbered.

"Nice doggy," Karen quavered.

"And this is Tyson ... and this is Lennox and this is ... " but the kids didn't wait to meet any more boxers.

"They're a bit too big for us to walk," said Jaz, backing away. "Sorry."

They legged it.

The yells of the man followed them down the street. "They're soft as butter really," he was shouting.

Behind him the massed growls of Bruno, Tyson, Lennox and their doggy mates rumbled like thunder.

CHAPTER 9
First meeting

Things picked up when they had their first meeting in their new den.

"Hey this is cool!" said Baz. "Seats! Cushions! A sofa! Even a rug and pictures. Cool!"

Tina and Kaz smirked with pride.

"We reckon our next mission should be to finish this off – you know, a light, a shelf, a pinboard for notices," said Kaz.

"I'm the leader, remember!" said Jaz. "And I say ..."

Everyone waited.

"I say we get this placed organised – a shelf, a light, notice board, that sort of thing. Okay?"

Everyone agreed and got busy.

Ten minutes later they were all happily at work when

All the gang stared and stopped. Eyes popping, hearts stopping, they looked at each other.

"What was THAT?" asked Baz. He looked all ready to start the Not So Famous Four synchronised tremble.

"That sound again!" said Tina. "We heard it before. I think it's a ghost."

"Or a spaceship engine," suggested Baz.

"Or a poor trapped animal screaming for help," said Karen, tearfully.

"Our next mission ..." announced Jaz, "is to discover the secret of that sound. Now listen carefully, where is it coming from?"

CHAPTER 10
The deserted warehouse

They sat still and held their breath.

"I can hear thumps," whispered Kaz.

"That's your heart beating, you twit," hissed her brother.

But he was wrong. After a minute, they could all hear distant thumps and scrapings. Then a yell. And then that unearthly screech again.

This time they *did* do their Not So Famous synchronised tremble. Kaz and Tina clutched each other. Baz shivered. Jaz tried to keep his cool but his face was pale.

"It's coming from next door," Tina said. "It's coming from the deserted warehouse!"

"It's okay," said Kaz, some time later. By this time they had calmed down a little – though they had been forced to eat all their emergency supplies of chocolate and cola before they had begun to feel better. "I know what to do. I've read all the Famous Five books."

She stood up straight and put on her bossiest look. "All we do is sneak out at ... about midnight and keep watch on the warehouse all through the night. That's exactly what the Famous Five would do. Now remember to bring your torches."

"Not so quick, kiddo!" said Jaz. "I'm the leader and I'm the oldest and I say ..."

Everyone waited.

"I say ... No. No way. No how. No."

"Awwwww ..." whined Kaz. "It's not fair ..."

"Look, little sister," said Jaz. "There is no way you're going to hang around at midnight ..."

"The Famous Five did," Karen pouted.

"The Famous Five didn't live round here," said Jaz. "It isn't safe."

Kaz stuck her lower lip out, folded her arms and sulked. Her face got redder.

"Sulk alert," said Jaz. "Megasulk! Tears and tantrums next. Everyone stand back!"

"I've got an idea," said Tina. Nobody asked her what it was but she went on anyway. "Kaz can stay the night at my house. She's allowed. And we can keep watch on the deserted warehouse from my bedroom window. That's what we should do. What about that then?"

Karen stopped in mid sob. She looked interested.

"Can I?" she asked.

"Just wait a minute," said Jaz. "I'm the leader and I say ..." Karen held her breath. "I say ... Why doesn't Kaz stay the night with Tina? You can both keep an eye on the deserted warehouse from there." Karen did a little hop of delight. Jaz thought for a moment. "And Baz can stay at my house and we can deal with important club matters."

"Like the badges?" asked Baz.

"Exactly!" said Jaz.

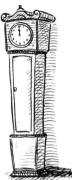

"It doesn't seem fair," said Baz. "Here we are while those two girls get to keep watch on the spooks." But he didn't really mind all that much. He was very proud of the badges.

He had also made some signs:

"Just write KEEP OUT," said Jaz, "and come and help with these identity cards. These are going to be so cool. Now let's think of some passwords."

Meanwhile at Tina's house, Kaz was peering through the window. "Still nothing," she sighed. "Your turn now."

Tina put down her comic. "Okay. Be sure to fill in our record of observations," she said.

Karen sighed again and picked up the notebook.

"BORING!" said Kaz. Detective work was proving to be something of a disappointment. "Nothing's happened at all. Not a sound. Not a thing."

There was no telly in Tina's room. They had already had their midnight feast and it was still only ten past nine. "Think I'll go to sleep for a bit," Kaz sighed. "Wake me up when it's my turn again."

The hours passed. The two girls took turns. One watched for an hour or so, one slept. Then they changed over.

Tina added details to the log.

Warehouse deserted and dark. Some tatty bits of curtain (black!) at some windows.

A spider plant (dead!) hanging at one window. ~~Quit~~ Quiet. No sign of life. Weird. It's dark now. No one on the streets. No traffic. No sounds. It feels as if I'm the only person in the world. Everything looks different as it gets darker and later.

Kaz was snuffling and squeaking in her sleep. She was dreaming. In her dream a screeching spook was chasing her. It was getting closer. It had hold of her! It was shaking her and calling her name ... "Kaz, Kaz, Kaz!" Karen opened her eyes and blinked herself awake. Tina was shaking her.

"Oh it's you," Kaz muttered. "I thought ..."

"Quick!" said Tina. "Get up. I've been trying to wake you for ages. Come and look. Now!"

Karen stumbled out of bed and both girls crouched behind the curtains and held their breath. They looked at each other, then pressed their noses against the window to get a better look. Tina was making notes. "Wait till the others hear about this!" she breathed.

CHAPTER 12
Another meeting

"We'll start the meeting now," said Jaz. "We've got loads of stuff to show you." He plonked a carrier bag full of papers on the packing case. "Look. Badges. Identity cards."

"But ..." said Tina.

"What do you think of those then?" said Baz.

"Great," said Tina, "but ..."

"And we've made signs too. Look!" said Baz.

"Good but ..."

"BUT WE'VE FOUND AN ADVENTURE!" yelled Kaz. "Listen to us!"

"Calm down," sighed Jaz. "I'm the leader and I'm the oldest and I say ... it's time to report back about your stake out."

Tina brought out her notebook and flipped the pages back importantly. "Seven pm. Nothing happened. The warehouse was quiet. Deserted. At the window a curtain ..."

"Fast forward to the action," said Kaz. "They can read the rest later."

"We heard a squeal," said Tina.

"A squeal of brakes," said Kaz.

"A van arrived."

"A black van."

"We couldn't read the number plate but it had Trans ... something written on it and ..."

"... and on the back door a glowing painting of a skull. A skull!"

"Out of the van came several figures."

"Tall they were and weird. Dressed in black. Long hair. Some wore hats. One wore a cloak!"

"They carried boxes."

"Big boxes. Big black boxes."

"They took them into the warehouse. Then the van was moved and everything went quiet again. We made a note of the time. Midnight."

"What do you think of that!" said Kaz. She folded her arms in triumph.

CHAPTER 13

"I think they're smugglers, or pirates," said Kaz. "They're bringing in their boxes of contraband and hiding them in the deserted warehouse."

"We're hundreds of miles from the sea," Jaz objected.

"Exactly!" said Kaz. "They think no one will suspect them of smuggling here. Or they could be robbers with boxes of stolen goods or kidnappers or ..."

"I've got it!" yelled Baz. "Wait there. Back in a tick."

It was several ticks but eventually he was back. He was clutching a videotape.

"Watch this," he said, "and all will be revealed."

The Four crept into Tina's house and put the video on as quietly as they could. Tina turned the sound right down. Next door, her Dad was snoring. The walls rumbled.

"He could snore for England," said Jaz.

"Sssh!" said Tina. "The video's starting."

"Oh," said Kaz, disappointed. "Black and white. Boring!"

The title came up written in gothic script and dripping with blood. It said:

Count Dracula

"Ooh!" said Kaz. "I don't like ..."

"She's not allowed to watch horror videos," said Jaz, reaching for the off switch.

"Just watch for five minutes," said Baz. "Then you'll get the idea."

The film started.

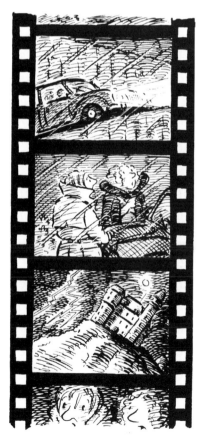

It was dark. Rain sheeted down. Storm clouds gathered. A couple were driving an old fashioned car through remote mountains. It broke down.

"Stay in the car!" Kaz advised them but of course they got out and started stumbling through the countryside. "Don't these people know anything?" Kaz sighed.

A spooky castle was suddenly illuminated by a flash of lightning. "Ooooh!" wailed Karen. "Don't go there!"

But of course that's exactly where they did go. They wandered right past the fiercest stone eagles you have ever seen, swung back an enormous iron gate and walked up to the massive door. They rang the bell.

The travellers listened as shuffling steps approached the door. There was the sound of rattling chains and the clanking of massive bolts being drawn back. A key was turned with a loud, grating noise. Then slowly, creakily, the door swung open.

The two travellers stared.

First they saw a pair of strange old boots. On top of that - two very long thin legs, then a coat - long, flapping, old fashioned and then ... the face - white and dusty, unsmiling.

"You rang?" said the strange figure. Then he opened the door wide. "Come in!" Even his voice was creaky.

"No don't go in. Don't!" Kaz warned them.

But in they went. "Excuse us for disturbing you ..." the travellers stammered, "but we've had a bit of trouble with our car."

Inside the castle there was a distinct lack of electricity. The odd candle glimmered half-heartedly. At the top of the stairs a cloaked figure stood. He turned to the camera, white-faced, evil-eyed ...

"Good evening." A slow, threatening sneer of a smile revealed very pointy teeth. "I am Count Dracula." Behind him lay a long black coffin. Outside, another flash of lightning lit up the castle.

"Get the idea?" asked Baz, pressing the pause button. "Vampires! We've got vampires next door!"

CHAPTER 14
Everything you ever wanted to know about vampires

"It all fits in," said Jaz. "Yes, it makes sense. Vampires."

"They only come out at night," said Tina. "They wear black ..."

"They wear capes and those boxes you saw were probably coffins," added Baz.

"The van has Trans ... something written on it. That was probably Transylvania – where Dracula comes from."

Tina added, "The wails and screeches are the cries of their poor terrorised victims!"

Kaz went white as a spook. "Oh noooo!" she wailed. "We've got vampires next door. What are we going to do?"

"I don't like it!" cried Kaz. "This is not the sort of adventure I wanted. It's not fair. First we don't get a dog and now ..."

"It'll be okay," said Baz.

"No it WON'T!" she shrieked. "I wanted kidnapped princes in towers, a mad scientist maybe. I didn't want vampires! Nasty blood-sucking, scary, killer vampires!" she shuddered.

"They can't touch us," Baz reassured her. "All we need is page 39 of this book. Look." He opened the book, turned to page 39 and showed them.

EVERYTHING YOU EVER WANTED TO KNOW ABOUT VAMPIRES

The following is all you need to know about how to protect yourself from vampires.

Remember vampires are only dangerous at night. They are powerless in the daytime. A beam of strong sunlight makes them crumble.

Vampires are terrified of religious objects.

Garlic is excellent protection against vampires. We advise the wearing of a string of garlic around the neck. Failing that, carry some garlic in your pocket.

Vampires can be killed by a stake through the heart.

"We'll watch the rest of the video – to see if we can pick up any other tips," said Jaz, settling back on to the sofa. "Not you kiddo," he said to Kaz. "You can tidy the den."

Kaz was sulky. She wasn't happy about this adventure. She wasn't happy about not being allowed to watch the video. She wasn't happy about having watched the bit of video she had seen. She felt sulky and shivery and scared. And she wasn't happy about being the one left to tidy the den. Tidying the den just wasn't the same all by yourself.

She sat and sulked.

After a while she started to arrange things on the shelf. She copied out the page from the vampire book. She headed it Protection From Vampires (hints) and stuck it up on the notice board. She felt a bit safer now.

The shelf was still pretty empty. "We need to brighten it up," she thought as she polished the jam jar she had found to use as a pencil jar. Then, of course, she knew exactly what the den needed to brighten it up. A jam jar of flowers! She filled the jar with water and set off to find flowers.

CHAPTER 15
Karen's adventure

Now the streets where the Not So Famous Four live are not exactly overflowing with flowers. Some people had a few stunted but brave little specimens struggling in their patches of garden, but most people seemed to go in for crops of crisp packets, or the occasional chip paper. After ten minutes all she had gathered were a few grubby daisies and a dandelion, which just floated weakly around in the jam jar. Of course there was the privet between the den and the warehouse ... The privet was in a rare state of flower. Clusters of little white flowers waved in the wind. They almost seemed to be waving to her. But nothing would make Karen go one step nearer the warehouse than she had to. On the other hand, she could see the white clumps of flowers twinkling at her. She could smell their sweet dizzying scent.

They were so near. She could grab a clump and be back in two minutes. "And it is daytime," she said to herself. "Vampires are powerless in the daytime. And I have read page 39 so I do know how to protect myself ... Won't the others be sick when they hear I've been right up to the deserted warehouse. They think they're so big watching their silly video. Wait till they hear what I've done!"

She pulled herself up to her full height and gave the deserted warehouse a very hard stare. "Vampires are powerless in the daytime," she chanted. "Vampires are powerless ..."

Off she went towards the deserted warehouse and the vampires.

CHAPTER 16
A sighting

Ten minutes later she'd gathered a good clump and was feeling pretty pleased with herself. "Nothing to be scared about," she was thinking ... when the back door of the warehouse creaked open.

Kaz crouched in the privet bush and held her breath. A tall, thin figure in black peered out. He was wearing a big hat and dark glasses and a loose, black, flapping coat lined in deep blood red. The sun could not touch him.

Karen stuffed her fist in her mouth to stop herself screaming. Slowly the door swung wider and the man started to drag something out. He stayed in the shadows by the wall and dragged something behind him.

"One of his poor victims!" thought Karen. He dragged whatever it was into a corner of the yard and then turned round.

Karen, dizzy from the smell of the privet flowers and shaky with fear, held her breath, closed her eyes and prayed. "Please don't let him find me ..."

Meanwhile, in Tina's flat, the video was crawling towards its conclusion. A happy ending was beginning to appear inevitable. The travellers who had been very snappy and bad tempered with each other at first had finally discovered they loved each other.

"I could have told them that an hour ago!" Tina commented sagely.

The travellers had finally realised what everyone else had known since minute one of the video, Count Dracula was not to be trusted. "He is an evil vampire who has to be defeated," they said. The truth was dawning slowly. So was the day. The storm had died down and daylight was approaching. Now the travellers only had to discover what Baz, Jaz and Tina had been trying to tell them for ages.

"Open the curtains!" shouted Baz. "Let in the light!"

Eventually they did just that and Dracula dissolved into dust. The end.

"Not a bad film," said Jaz, rubbing his eyes. "Better go and find that pest of a sister now."

"She hasn't done much," said Tina, looking round the den.

"Probably sulking," said Jaz. "Kaz! Where are you?"

Silence.

"Come on kiddo. You can come out now. Abandon sulk."

Still nothing.

"Time to eat!" tempted Tina. "We've got KitKats!"

Still no Kaz.

Jaz began to look a bit worried. "Perhaps I shouldn't have left her by herself. Mum'll kill me."

"KAZ! Come on Kaz!"

"Right, everybody get searching for her."

They looked through Tina's house but apart from a couple of grumpy parents they found nothing.

They looked in the street. Nothing.

They looked in the alley. Nothing.

They even looked on the garage roof. Nothing.

It was while Baz was on the flat roof that he spotted something. "Jaz. Look at that ... that bush ... it seems to be moving ... breathing."

Between the den and the warehouse the privet bush shook and quivered.

Cautiously they approached the bush. They poked a stick at it. Tina pulled back a branch.

"Ooh!" squealed the bush.

Ten minutes, one Coke and two KitKats later, Karen felt strong enough to tell them what had happened. "I've seen him dragging out the remains of his victims," she shuddered. "He's stacked them up in the back yard. You're the leader," she said to Jaz, "what should we do?"

"Storm in to the rescue?" suggested Baz.

"Surround the warehouse with garlic?" added Tina.

"Run away?" suggested Kaz.

"I'm the leader," said Jaz, "and I say ..." He wrinkled his face in effort while he searched for the solution. "I say ... we tell the police. That's the sensible grown-up thing to do."

"The Famous Five never bothered telling the police," said Tina but she tagged on anyway as they went off to the police station.

CHAPTER 18
At the police station

The Four had never been in a police station before though they'd all seen a lot of them on the telly. Real life, as usual, was a bit of a disappointment. No burly officers came in dragging captured burglars. No one screamed and protested their innocence. There was not a single gun fired all the time they were there.

All there was was a small queue of people at a counter. There was an old lady who'd lost her purse, a man who'd lost his driving licence and a woman who'd lost her way.

The Four waited their turn and read the walls.

HAVE YOU SEEN THIS MAN?

'HAVE YOU SEEN THIS MAN?' was the question on one of the photos.

"No I haven't!" said Kaz. "And I don't want to. He looks like he's been blown apart and stuck together again." She didn't understand about photofit pictures and no one explained to her. They were too nervous waiting for their turn.

They looked straight ahead while Kaz read the walls out to them and asked questions.

Eventually they got to the front of the queue and a woman ignored them while she scribbled in a book.

"She's not a policewoman," hissed Tina. "She hasn't even got a uniform."

"Leave it to me," said Jaz. "Excuse me," he said in a very grown up and leader-type voice. "We want to see the Chief Constable."

"Name?" said the woman.

"Well we don't know his name, do we?" said Baz. "Chief Constable Something-or-other, I suppose."

"Your name?" sighed the woman.

"Jaz ... James Mayfield," said Jaz. "Look. This is urgent. We've found vampires!"

"Bats," said the woman.

"We are NOT!" said Kaz, indignantly. "We ..."

"Have you found bats?" asked the woman. "Vampire bats?"

"No," said Jaz, "real vampires. Real live vampires. Well, real live dead vampires if you see what I mean."

"They live next door to me," added Tina helpfully. "Next door to the chip shop."

"Vampires next door to the chip shop," sighed the woman. "Is this some sort of joke? Clear off."

CHAPTER 19
Finding evidence

"So much for the grown up, sensible approach," said Baz. "They never believe kids."

"We need proof," said Jaz. "That's all we need. Hard evidence."

Kaz did not suggest she hung around the warehouse at midnight. She was learning.

"We'll take it in turns to observe and keep notes," Jaz ordered. "Then we just take our notebooks along to the police as evidence." He started drawing up a rota. "During the day we can sit on the garage roof and keep a lookout. At night, Kaz and Tina can keep watch from Tina's bedroom window." He stuck the rota up on the wall.

ROTA

Morning watch — Baz
Afternoon watch — Baz
Evening watch — Kaz and Tina

"You don't seem to have given yourself many shifts," objected Baz.

"Someone's got to take charge. I have to supervise," said Jaz, lying back. "While Baz is on first shift, the rest of you can carry on sorting out the den."

"We should start looking for things to protect us from the vampires," said Baz.

"Listen, I'm the oldest and I'm the leader," said Jaz, "and I say ..." but they'd guessed that he was going to say they should start looking for things to protect themselves from vampires and they were off.

Tina and Kaz set off for their houses to see what they could find. Baz scrambled up on to the roof to keep watch and Jaz ... Jaz plugged in his Walkman. "I'll just stay here and do all the thinking and planning," he said, lying back and closing his eyes. "It's a tough job but someone's got to do it."

He was in the middle of a very important dream when Kaz woke him. "We've got loads of stuff," she said, "Look!"

Tina had a small, white, crinkly onion-type thing clutched in her hand. "It's garlic!" she said. "The real thing. My Dad uses it when he makes moussaka and kebabs and stuff. Vampires are powerless against it."

Jaz looked a little doubtful. He'd never seen garlic before, but at first glance it didn't look all that deadly.

Karen had been less successful. "Mum doesn't go in for fancy food," she explained, "but I found these at the back of the cupboard." She proudly presented her finds – a packet of mix-your-own Garlic and Mushroom Sauce (just add water) and a jar of mixed herbs.

"Better than nothing, I suppose," said Jaz.

"I've got more!" said Kaz and proudly held out ... a light bulb. "It's a daylight simulation bulb. Don't you see? If it's dark we can put this bulb in and the vampires will crumble away in the daylight!"

"Instant Vampire Crumble," said Jaz. "We can eat it with the sauce. No seriously, well done, kiddo. Well done."

"It's your turn to take over!" yelled Baz. He was getting a bit grumpy up on the roof all by himself. "I'm off duty now. I'm going to the corner shop for some chocolate. Oh by the way, I saw absolutely nothing – except some sacks stacked near the warehouse. Was that what was dragged out and stashed in the corner? They look a bit like ordinary bin bags to me." He gave Kaz a withering glance and set off for the corner shop.

CHAPTER 20
An adventure for Baz

Baz decided to stay at the corner shop for as long as possible. He didn't want to have to share his chocolate with the others. He wasn't feeling very generous to them. For one thing he'd been on duty all by himself all morning. For another thing he was due to be on duty all by himself all afternoon.

He decided to stay away from the den as long as possible so Jaz would be forced to do a bit of the work. He perched on the edge of a litter bin and ate his chocolate, casually reading all the notices in the shop window. He had a little giggle at:

Comfy sofa for sale.

by old lady with
sagging bottom.

enquiries:

HAVE FUN!
Join your local archery
club.
We are targetting teenagers
and old age pensioners.

Tel: 003 25 6 211

... and then his attention was drawn by:

DOGSITTER
REQUIRED.

Dogsitter! Was this the answer to Baz's prayers? He could just imagine himself turning up at the den in the afternoon pulling a big, faithful, loyal guard dog behind him.

At last they would really be the Famous Five and it would all be thanks to him. He imagined the scene and a warm glow of satisfaction spread through him. He scribbled the address down and set off. But first he ran round to the den. "I'll be late back. Take my shift will you

Jaz?" he called. "I'm just off to pick up a dog," he said casually and before they could ask any questions he was off, fired by hope and a sense of heroism.

"I'll get a dog this time," he said to himself, "or perish in the attempt!"

●

CHAPTER 21
The guard dog

It was over an hour before Baz got back to the den. Jaz was hard at work, on guard on the garage roof. He was resting his head on the notebook and snoring gently. Karen and Tina skipped up to Baz.

"Have you got a dog? Have you? Have you?" they trilled.

Baz shuffled his feet and blushed.

"Oh no," said Jaz, opening his eyes. "Have you chickened out again? If you want something doing round here you have to do it yourself."

"As a matter of fact I have got a dog," said Baz.

"So where is it then?" Jaz sneered.

"Here!" said Baz and put his hand into his jacket and pulled out ...

a very furry,

very quivery,

very very very small ... creature.

"Aaaw!" sighed Kaz. "A guinea pig. How cute!"

"It's a dog," said Baz indignantly. "A miniature Yorkshire Terrier, actually."

"I can just see that protecting us from the crooks and the smugglers ... not to mention the vampires," sneered Jaz.

"Look at the thing."

It was tiny and long haired. It looked like someone's pet wig. It had a teeny little nose that sniffed nervously like a bunny and two little button eyes practically covered in hair. It stood in Baz's hand and shivered.

"Well I think it's sweet," said Tina kindly. "What's its name?"

"Moppet," mumbled Baz.

"Mophead!" crowed Jaz. "The dog that looks like a dishmop. The fierce and loyal dog that is going to make us into The Famous Five. Ha! You're on duty again Baz," and Jaz sloped off to read a comic and listen to his Walkman.

CHAPTER 22
Moppet

Baz tried his best but he couldn't persuade Moppet to stay on the roof with him. Moppet was a very nervous little dog and the height seemed to bother it.

Kaz and Tina took pity on it. "Come to us, Moppet. Come to us! Let it play down here with us. It's scared of heights."

Moppet was so scared it was pathetic. It stood and it shook and it shivered. It made a small wet whimpering like a particularly unheroic mouse.

"Okay," said Baz. "But be careful. I'm responsible for it." Baz was a boy who took his responsibilities seriously.

Tina and Kaz tried training Moppet. They tried training it to fetch ...

Moppet sat still

To sit ...

Moppet walked off.

To beg ...

Moppet fell over.

Then they got fed up and left it running around in the yard.

From on top of the garage Baz could see Moppet chasing a butterfly and looking decidedly unlike a guard dog. It didn't run and bark. It sort of ... skipped and squeaked. It was a great disappointment. It was scrabbling in the privet hedge now, wrestling with a sweet wrapper. It looked as if the sweet wrapper would win.

A sudden gust of wind picked up the wrapper and Moppet skittered after it.

"Hey come back," yelled Baz. But too late. Moppet had gone ...

through the hedge ...

over the yard ...

and into the deserted warehouse.

CHAPTER 23
A vote

"Moppet!" screamed Baz. "Come back!"

Too late. Moppet had found the tiniest crack in the big old door to the warehouse. Flattening himself, he squeezed right through and into the deserted warehouse - into the vampire's lair.

"Oh no!" wailed Baz. "We've got to do something. Jaz!"

Jaz called a meeting.

"All we can do," said Tina, "is wait. Moppet will probably come back sooner or later."

"If the vampires don't get him first," added Kaz.

"You don't understand," said Baz. "That dog belongs to an old lady. I promised I'd guard it with my life. She has to go to hospital and queue up for hours and hours and she wanted to know Moppet was in safe hands while she was out ..." Baz was almost in tears. "I can't go back to a sick old lady and tell her I've lost her little pet - to vampires! We've got to go in and rescue Moppet."

Jaz took a deep breath. "Well I'm the oldest and I'm the leader and I say ..."

Everyone waited.

"I say ... No. No rescue. No way. No chance! You just go round to the lady and explain you couldn't help it."

"I can help it," said Baz, "and I will. By myself if the rest of you are too chicken! Who's brave enough to help me? Who's brave enough to help a poor, helpless, frightened little dog?"

There was a silence.

Then an unexpected squeak from Kaz. She surprised herself as much as anyone when she said, "I don't think we can leave Moppet in there ... without protection."

"Vote. Let's take a vote," said Baz. "All in favour of rescuing Moppet hands up." He stuck his own hand in the air.

Then Karen shakily raised her hand too. She couldn't bear to think of that poor, small dog in there all alone.

When Tina saw Kaz ... she held her hand up too. Which left Jaz.

"Oh all right, I suppose," he said reluctantly. Then, taking charge, he gave his orders. "Gather up all the equipment – everything to protect ourselves from vampires. Get a move on. We want to be in and out of there before it gets dark."

CHAPTER 24
Into the vampire's lair

BANG! BANG! BANG! Baz thumped his fist on the door, and BANG! Kaz added her own, slightly more timid, contribution.

The Four held their breath and their weapons tightly. Their weapons were:

- the garlic (which Tina held aloft in front of her),

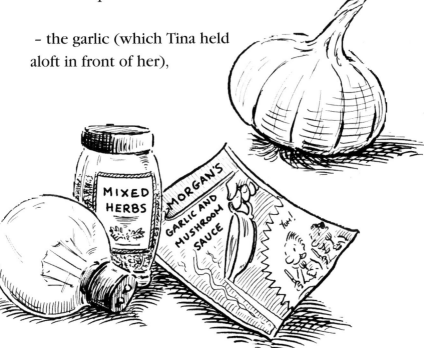

- the herbs, the garlic sauce and the bulb (which Baz and Kaz held more in hope and desperation than anything else),

– and a cricket stump
(which Jaz had brought
along in case he needed
to drive a stake through
a vampire's heart).

They waited, one minute ...
two minutes ...
three minutes.

"No one's coming. Too bad," said Jaz with some relief. "Come on we might as well go home."

"No," said Baz. "Listen."

They could hear someone groaning in the warehouse ... and something else, a shuffling. Someone or something was shuffling towards the door.

Now three of the Four had watched the vampire film and three of the Four should have known that now was the time to turn tail and run, but ... one of them felt responsible for Moppet.

I must stay and rescue poor Mophead.

One felt responsible for the others.

One felt responsible for Karen.

The fourth was rooted to the spot in terror.

So they stayed where they were and listened to the sound of rattling chains and the clanking of massive bolts being pulled back. A key was turned with a loud grating noise. Then slowly and creakily, the door opened.

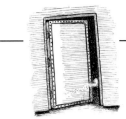

CHAPTER 25
The door opens ...

The Four shivered, shook and stared. What did they see? They saw:

a pair of very dusty, black, odd and old fashioned boots

then

a pair of long, very thin legs

then

a black flowing cloak lined in blood red silk

and

a face, a deathly white face with bloodshot eyes.

It was the face of a creature that had not seen sunshine for many a day.

The figure stooped and peered at them. Then it spoke. "You banged?" it said in a hollow and eerie voice.

A grey cloud covered the sun. Suddenly it was darker, and rainy.

"We should leave now, quick!" said Tina. "Let's leg it!"

"What about Mophead?" whispered Baz. "I promised we'd take care of him."

"Safety in numbers," hissed Jaz. "We all stay," and he clutched his cricket stump tightly, took a deep breath and tried to speak in his loudest most leader-like voice. "Excuse us for disturbing you but we've had a bit of an accident with our ..." Suddenly it all sounded dreadfully familiar to him and he couldn't go on.

Kaz took over. "Dog," she managed to squeak and then her nerve failed too.

"Come in," intoned the sinister figure and he swung the door open wide for them.

Hypnotised by fear, the Four did as they were told and then there they were, inside the deserted warehouse. It was every bit as weird as they'd imagined.

Bare floors.

Dim lights.

Strange paintings on the walls.

Boxes everywhere.

Odd noises ... moanings, squeaking and ...
a familiar yapping.

"Mophead!" shrieked Baz and he pushed open the next door. Then he stood transfixed.

"What is it?" asked Jaz. "What can you see?"

Then he pushed through and he too fell silent.

CHAPTER 26
A terrible sight

In the middle of a vast empty room stood four strange figures. Their faces were illuminated by a strange glow. Behind them the rest of the room was in darkness. Dark shapes of huge boxes loomed in the shadows. All around them swirled a dense fog.

Through the clouds of mist, Baz could see one of the strange people had hold of Moppet. The Not So Famous Four stood as if turned to stone. It was worse than they could have imagined.

The one behind them spoke. "We said we needed some fresh blood and look what I've found on the doorstep ..."

Hearing this, Kaz came to life. She woke from her trance of frozen fear and with an ear-piercing shriek, she turned and ran, pushing over the pale-faced figure behind her and throwing her Garlic and Mushroom Sauce at him.

Tina was on her heels, leaping over the knocked-down figure and screaming fit to bust. Jaz wasn't far behind. But Baz ... Baz decided to make a grab for Mophead before running.

He jumped towards the strange figures in the fog, grabbed Mophead and got ready to run when all of a sudden he stopped. "Oh ..." he said, "I see."

CHAPTER 27
Vampire crumble

Kaz, Jaz and Tina were nearly at the door when they noticed Baz hadn't made it. Although she was possibly the most terrified of all of them, Kaz did not hesitate. She turned right round and ran back to rescue her friend.

"Oh no!" groaned Jaz, but he couldn't leave his sister behind so back he went with his heart sinking. Tina dragged along at the back.

"Okay. Let him go!" yelled Jaz in the bravest, biggest voice he could manage.

"Or you're crumble," added Kaz, brandishing the light bulb.

"Hey, what's the big deal?" said the pale-faced figure who was now stroking Mophead. "We wouldn't hurt your guinea pig."

"It's a dog," said Baz indignantly. "Hang on," he added to Jaz, who was shaking his cricket stump very threateningly. "I think we may have made a mistake. Just calm down and look."

They looked.

What did they see?

They saw ...

four young men
  with pale faces,
    dark clothes and ...
      guitars.

They saw
a spotlight,
a smoke machine
and boxes of musical
equipment –
speakers, amplifiers, keyboards.
All in big coffin-like boxes.

Someone turned the smoke machine off. The mist that it had made gradually drifted away. Someone else turned off the spotlights and turned on the main lights. Everything looked very different now.

"Ah," said Kaz, touching the keyboard.

AWWWWWWWww

went the keyboard.

"Oh," said Jaz, suddenly feeling very small, very young and not at all like a leader. "You're a rock group, rehearsing ..."

CHAPTER 28

... solve the mystery

"That's what we are," said one of the young musicians. "I'm Jake and this is my band. We've got the music. We've got the image. We've got the equipment ... even the dry ice – makes a great effect, doesn't it? All we need now is a name for the band."

"Yeah," said another, "we were just saying how we need some like new ideas – you know, fresh blood, young ideas. We're desperate to find an unusual name. You turned up at just the right time. Let's hear all your brilliant ideas."

A long silence fell.

"Er, what sort of image were you trying to get with the name?" asked Jaz eventually.

"Creepy," said one of the musicians, "But friendly too – and easy to remember."

"What about 'The Earwigs'?" suggested Tina, "or 'Spiders' – they're pretty creepy ..."

"Daddy Long Legs," suggested Baz, looking at the long, thin legs of the keyboard player.

"Not bad," said Jake, "but not different enough."

Kaz was looking bewildered. She still had hold of her light bulb. She wasn't entirely convinced that all danger was past. "You mean you're just ordinary – well, weird but ordinary people?" she muttered. "You mean you're not the vampires next door."

"Sssh!" hissed Jaz. He was embarrassed by the mistake they had made.

"The Vampires Next Door!" said the keyboard player. "Vampires Next Door – that's it. It's creepy but funny and friendly being next door like and ..."

"And people will remember it," added Jake. "It's a good name."

"And you look like vampires anyway," added Tina, "you're all so pale."

"Most of our work is done at night," Jake said. "We don't get to do a lot of sunbathing!"

"You could carry your equipment in coffins," suggested Jaz. He was feeling better by the minute. "You could write Transylvania on the back of your black van. Or is that written on your van already?" He looked at Tina, remembering what she had written in her report.

"It says 'Ford Transit'," said the drummer. "We could change it easily. I knew you kids would have fresh ideas. This is all great."

"Now we'll do something for you," said Jake. "We'll give you our very first publicity poster with our new name on."

He gave them a big, glossy black and white poster of the group and on it, in blood red, he wrote:

So the Not So Famous Four (or four and a half if you count Moppet) pinned their first trophy onto the wall in the den.

"It looks great!" said Kaz.

"Just wait till they're famous and we can tell everyone at school about it," said Tina, tucking into a celebratory KitKat.

"But now the mystery is solved, the adventure's over and it's time to take Mophead back," said Baz sadly. "And then what?"

They all turned to Jaz.

"Well I'm the oldest and I'm the leader," he said. "And I say ..."

Everyone waited.

"I say we all get busy looking for another adventure!"

So that's what they did – but that, of course, is another story.